STORY BY
LIZ ROSENBERG

MONSTER MAMA

ILLUSTRATIONS BY
STEPHEN GAMMELL

PAPERSTAR

The Putnam & Grosset Group

Patrick Edward was a wonderful boy, but his mother was a monster. She lived in a big cave at the back of the house.

Sometimes she painted, sometimes she gardened, and sometimes she tossed Patrick Edward lightly up and down in the air, for fun. He called her Monster Mama.

Her bad moods terrified the neighborhood.

Still, she had the sweetest touch
in the world when Patrick Edward
ran a fever.

She taught him how to roar, how to jump and climb, how to cast a spell that could put almost anyone to sleep.

Patrick Edward was fearless, like her. She told him, "Always use your powers for good, never for evil."

On rainy days when she drove him
to school, she hid herself in a big cloak
and hood.

When he invited friends over, she baked cookies for them and watched secretly from the cave. She never introduced herself to Patrick Edward's teachers or his piano instructor.

"They don't need to meet me," she said.

So Patrick Edward passed out the cookies himself and learned how to make friends on his own.

One day Patrick Edward's mother told him to pick out something lovely for dessert. "Something with strawberries," she called after him.

He decided to try the new market across town.
He picked out some lovely strawberry tarts.

But out in the parking lot, three big boys
circled him.

"Yum," said the first boy, grabbing the
grocery bag. Another boy waved a baseball bat.

Patrick Edward was unafraid. "Creeps," he
sang out, snatching back the bag. The boys
ran after him.

They chased him down the street and into
an empty lot. "Villains, farewell!" howled
Patrick Edward.

He jumped over a creek, flew through
the woods, and bounded up the side of a
small mountain. But the three boys
caught up.

"We'll show him who's boss," they said,
so Patrick Edward chanted the spell that
would make them fall asleep. But though
he said the words in the right order, and
looked them straight in the eye, those boys
couldn't be charmed.

They gobbled up Patrick Edward's
lovely dessert and tied him to a tree with
a piece of twine. They threw his cap off
the mountain and tossed the paper bag after it.

"Lizards," Patrick Edward said scornfully.
"Death to all tyrants!"

"Aw, your mother wears army boots,"
snarled the biggest boy.

"What?" said Patrick Edward.

"You heard me," said the boy. The other
two smirked.

"YOU LEAVE MY MOTHER OUT OF THIS!"
Patrick Edward roared, so loudly the whole
mountain rang. He broke the baseball bat like
a loaf of stale bread and tossed the pieces
over his shoulder.

Then he chased the boys back down the mountain, and through the woods. His eyes glowed and his laughter was truly monstrous.

Who knows what might have happened next—
but Monster Mama heard the echoes of his roar.
She zoomed out of her cave like a fast-moving
freight train and sailed over the creek in one
graceful leap.

"Who is *that*?" shrieked the boys.
"Let's skip the introductions,"
Patrick Edward's mother howled.
"Pick up that bag!"
    The three boys scampered after it.

"Don't forget the hat," she snapped. They
found it hanging from a bramble bush.

"And who broke the baseball bat?" Her eyes
had little red flames in them.

Patrick Edward blushed.

"And I still want something lovely for
dessert!" she thundered, and she marched
all the boys back home—

where they feverishly sifted and stirred
and baked a strawberry tea cake with
French whipped cream on top.

At the supper table, Patrick Edward said,
"Strength is for the wise, not the reckless.
—More cake, please," he added. The three
boys had second helpings.

Monster Mama carried out the dishes.
Patrick Edward stacked them.

"No matter where you go, or what you do," she told him, "I will be there. Because I am your mother, even if I am a monster—and I love you."

As soon as it grew dark, Patrick Edward walked the boys to the gate.

"Your mother is something else," they told him admiringly.

"It runs in the family," answered Patrick Edward.

To my son, Eli, a wonderful boy
and to my mother, the original Monster Mama

L.R.

To everyone that cared,
and especially to those who still do...

S.G.

Printed on recycled paper

Text copyright © 1993 by Liz Rosenberg
Illustrations copyright © 1993 by Stephen Gammell
All rights reserved. This book, or parts thereof, may not be
reproduced in any form without permission in writing from the publisher.
A PaperStar Book, published in 1997 by The Putnam & Grosset Group,
200 Madison Avenue, New York, NY 10016. PaperStar Books and
the PaperStar logo are trademarks of The Putnam Berkley Group, Inc.
Originally published in 1993 by Philomel Books.
Published simultaneously in Canada.
Printed in the United States of America.

Library of Congress Cataloging-in-Publication Data
Rosenberg, Liz.
Monster mama/by Liz Rosenberg, illustrated by Stephen Gammell.
p.   cm.
Summary: Patrick Edward's fierce monster mother helps him deal
with some obnoxious bullies.
[1. Mothers and sons—Fiction.   2. Bullies—Fiction.]
I. Gammell, Stephen. ill. II. Title.
PZ7.R71894Mo   1993   [E]—dc20   91-46825 CIP AC

ISBN 0-698-11429-0
10 9 8 7 6 5 4 3 2 1